THE CHILDREN'S
Book of Virtues

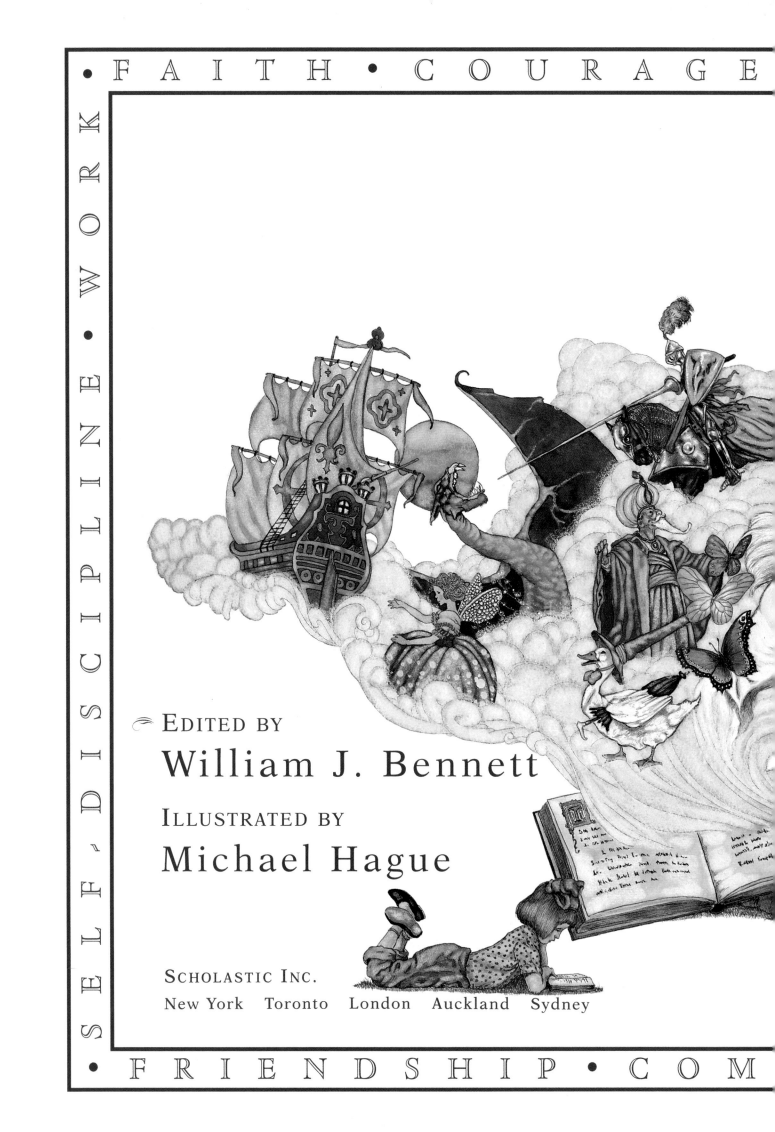

FAITH • COURAGE

WORK • SELF-DISCIPLINE • COMPASSION

~ EDITED BY
# William J. Bennett

ILLUSTRATED BY
Michael Hague

SCHOLASTIC INC.
New York   Toronto   London   Auckland   Sydney

FRIENDSHIP • COM

THE CHILDREN'S
Book of Virtues

This book is a work of fiction. Names, characters, places, and incidents either are products of the author's imagination or are used fictitiously. Any resemblance to actual events or locales or persons, living or dead, is entirely coincidental.

ISBN 0-590-97266-9

Text copyright © 1995 by William J. Bennett.
Illustrations copyright © 1995 by Michael Hague.
All rights reserved. Published by Scholastic Inc., 555 Broadway, New York, NY 10012, by arrangement with Simon & Schuster.

12 11 10 9 8 7 6   7 8 9/9 0 1/0

Printed in the U.S.A.

First Scholastic printing, September 1996   2 3

"The Indian Cinderella," reprinted from *Canadian Wonder Tales* by Cyrus Macmillan, by permission of the Estate of the author and The Bodley Head, publisher.

INTRODUCTION

The impetus for this book was a comment I began to hear over and over soon after the original *Book of Virtues* was published: "Our family loves these stories, but it's too bad there are no pictures!" As every parent knows, the chances of enticing a child to climb into (and stay in) your lap increase considerably when you hold out a picture book—as opposed to an eight-hundred-page anthology. So I was delighted when Simon & Schuster agreed to produce an illustrated edition of stories and poems selected from *The Book of Virtues* especially for younger children.

There was no question in my wife's mind as to who should paint the images to accompany these time-honored verses and tales. Elayne had passed more than a few story hours with our sons, John and Joe, at her side, reading books illustrated by Michael Hague. When I told her about this project, she reached for the phone and began tracking down her favorite illustrator. Fortunately, Michael was available and willing, and the happy results fill the following pages. As you will see, his images have a vital spark that leads young minds toward the noble and gentle and fine. Words and pictures speak together of hearts and souls where virtues dwell. These stories and Michael Hague's pen make a great match.

Like the original anthology, this edition aims specifically at the time-honored task of the moral education of the young. Moral education—the training of heart and mind toward the good—involves many things. It involves rules and precepts—the *do's* and *don'ts* of life with others. It involves explicit training in good habits. And it involves the example of adults who, through their daily behavior, show children they take morality seriously.

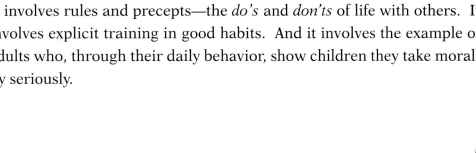

Along with precept, habit, and example, there is also the need for what we may call moral literacy. This collection is a "how to" book to help young children achieve such literacy. The stories and poems presented here can help them start to see what the virtues look like, what they are in practice, how to recognize them, and how they work. If we want our children to possess the traits of character we most admire—honesty and courage and compassion—we need to teach them what those traits are and why they deserve both admiration and allegiance.

It is never too early to begin the task. The stories in these pages can help build a first stock of examples illustrating what we perceive to be right or wrong, good or bad. They have stood the test of time in part because they are fascinating to young children. Nothing in recent years, on television or anywhere else, has improved on a good story that begins "Once upon a time . . ." But I believe they have stood the test of time for another reason. They appeal not only to children's imaginations but to their moral sense as well. They have the power to impress themselves upon young minds and remain as life-long guides.

And so the material in this book speaks without hesitation, without embarrassment, to the moral sense, to the souls of our children. Today we talk about how important it is to "have values," as if they were beads or a string of marbles in a pouch. But these stories speak to morality and virtues not as something to be possessed but as the core of human nature, not as something to *have* but as something to *be*, the most important thing to be. To dwell among these stories and verses is to put oneself, through the imagination, into a different place and time, a time when there was little doubt that children were essentially moral and spiritual beings, when the verities were the moral verities, when the central task of education was virtue. As we read these stories to and with our young children, we begin to acquaint them with the idea that it is the moral life, the life of virtue, that is worth living. We invite them to lift their young eyes. As St. Paul wrote, "Whatever is true, whatever is honorable, whatever is right, whatever is pure, whatever is lovely, whatever is of good repute, if there is any excellence and anything worthy of praise, let your mind dwell on these things."

I hope this book will help parents and young children dwell on these things together. ⌒

CONTENTS

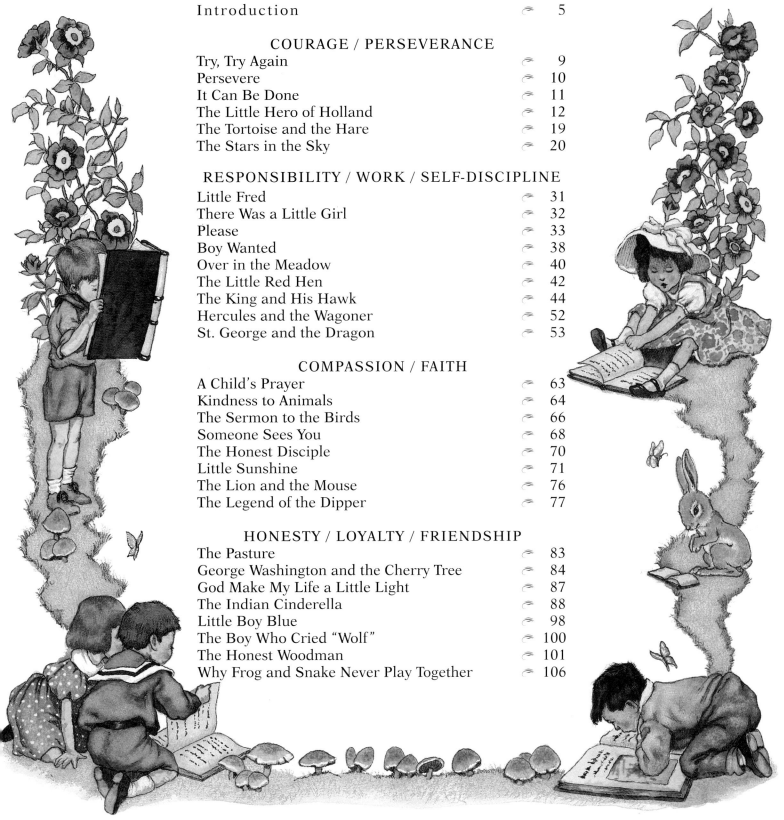

COURAGE
···
PERSEVERANCE

Try, Try Again

'Tis a lesson you should heed,
    Try, try again;
If at first you don't succeed,
    Try, try again;
Then your courage should appear,
For, if you will persevere,
You will conquer, never fear;
    Try, try again.

Persevere

Stick-to-it-iveness has a lot to do with getting the right answers in math, English, history, and life.

The fisher who draws in his net too soon,
  Won't have any fish to sell;
The child who shuts up his book too soon,
  Won't learn any lessons well.

If you would have your learning stay,
  Be patient—don't learn too fast;
The man who travels a mile each day,
  May get round the world at last.

It Can Be Done

Brave people think things through and ask, "Is this the best way to do this?"
Cowards, on the other hand, always say, "It can't be done."

The man who misses all the fun
Is he who says, "It can't be done."
In solemn pride he stands aloof
And greets each venture with reproof.
Had he the power he'd efface
The history of the human race;
We'd have no radio or motor cars,
No streets lit by electric stars;
No telegraph nor telephone,
We'd linger in the age of stone.
The world would sleep if things were run
By men who say, "It can't be done."

The Little Hero of Holland

⁁ ADAPTED FROM ETTA AUSTIN BLAISDELL
AND MARY FRANCES BLAISDELL

Here is the true story of a brave heart, one willing to hold on as long as it takes to get the job done.

Holland is a country where much of the land lies below sea level. Only great walls called dikes keep the North Sea from rushing in and flooding the land. For centuries the people of Holland have worked to keep the walls strong so that their country will be safe and dry. Even the little children know the dikes must be watched every moment, and that a hole no larger than your finger can be a very dangerous thing.

Many years ago there lived in Holland a boy named Peter. Peter's father was one of the men who tended the gates in the dikes, called sluices. He opened and closed the sluices so that ships could pass out of Holland's canals into the great sea.

One afternoon in the early fall, when Peter was eight years old, his mother called him from his play. "Come, Peter," she said. "I want you to go across the dike and take these cakes to your friend, the blind man. If you go quickly, and do not stop to play, you will be home again before dark."

The little boy was glad to go on such an errand, and started off with a light heart. He stayed with the poor blind man a little while to tell him about his walk along the dike and about the sun and the flowers and the ships far out at sea. Then he remembered his mother's wish that he should return before dark and, bidding his friend good-bye, he set out for home.

As he walked beside the canal, he noticed how the rains had swollen the waters, and how they beat against the side of the dike, and he thought of his father's gates.

"I am glad they are so strong," he said to himself. "If they gave way what would become of us? These pretty fields would be covered with water. Father always calls them the 'angry waters.' I suppose he thinks they are angry at him for keeping them out so long."

As he walked along he sometimes stopped to pick the pretty blue flowers that grew beside the road, or to listen to the rabbits' soft tread as they rustled through the grass. But oftener he smiled as he thought of his visit to the poor blind man who had so few pleasures and was always so glad to see him.

Suddenly he noticed that the sun was setting, and that it was growing dark. "Mother will be watching for me," he thought, and he began to run toward home.

Just then he heard a noise. It was the sound of trickling water! He stopped and looked down. There was a small hole in the dike, through which a tiny stream was flowing.

Any child in Holland is frightened at the thought of a leak in the dike.

Peter understood the danger at once. If the water ran through a little hole it would soon make a larger one, and the whole country would be flooded. In a moment he saw what he must do. Throwing away his flowers, he climbed down the side of the dike and thrust his finger into the tiny hole.

The flowing of the water was stopped!

"Oho!" he said to himself. "The angry waters must stay back now. I can keep them back with my finger. Holland shall not be drowned while I am here."

This was all very well at first, but it soon grew dark and cold. The little fellow shouted and screamed. "Come here; come here," he called. But no one heard him; no one came to help him.

It grew still colder, and his arm ached, and began to grow stiff and numb. He shouted again, "Will no one come? Mother! Mother!"

But his mother had looked anxiously along the dike road many times since sunset for her little boy, and now she had closed and locked the cottage door, thinking that Peter was spending the night with his blind friend, and that she would scold him in the morning for staying away from home without her permission.

Peter tried to whistle, but his teeth chattered with the

cold. He thought of his brother and sister in their warm beds, and of his dear father and mother. "I must not let them be drowned," he thought. "I must stay here until someone comes, if I have to stay all night."

The moon and stars looked down on the child crouching on a stone on the side of the dike. His head was bent, and his eyes were closed, but he was not asleep, for every now and then he rubbed the hand that was holding back the angry sea.

"I'll stand it somehow," he thought. So he stayed there all night keeping the water out.

Early the next morning a man going to work thought he heard a groan as he walked along the top of the dike. Looking over the edge, he saw a child clinging to the side of the great wall.

"What's the matter?" he called. "Are you hurt?"

"I'm keeping the water back!" Peter yelled. "Tell them to come quickly!"

The alarm was spread. People came running with shovels, and the hole was soon mended.

They carried Peter home to his parents, and before long the whole town knew how he had saved their lives that night. To this day, they have never forgotten the brave little hero of Holland.

The Tortoise and the Hare

⤲ A E S O P

We win many of life's rewards by learning how to hang in there and work till the very end.

A hare once made fun of a tortoise. "What a slow way you have!" he said. "How you creep along!"

"Do I?" said the tortoise. "Try a race with me and I'll beat you."

"What a boaster you are," said the hare. "But come! I will race with you. Whom shall we ask to mark off the finish line and see that the race is fair?"

"Let us ask the fox," said the tortoise.

The fox was very wise and fair. He showed them where they were to start, and how far they were to run.

The tortoise lost no time. He started out at once and jogged straight on.

The hare leaped along swiftly for a few minutes till he had left the tortoise far behind. He knew he could reach the mark very quickly, so he lay down by the road under a shady tree and took a nap.

By and by he awoke and remembered the race. He sprang up and ran as fast as he could. But when he reached the mark the tortoise was already there!

"Slow and steady wins the race," said the fox.

The Stars in the Sky

☞ ADAPTED FROM CAROLYN SHERWIN BAILEY, KATE DOUGLAS WIGGIN, AND NORA ARCHIBALD SMITH

This old English tale reminds us that the higher we reach, the longer and harder we have to try.

Once upon a time there was a little lass who wanted nothing more than to touch the stars in the sky. On clear, moonless nights she would lean out her bedroom window, gazing up at the thousand tiny lights scattered across the heavens, wondering what it would be like to hold one in her hand.

One warm summer evening, a night when the Milky

Way shone more brightly than ever before, she decided she couldn't stand it any longer—she just had to touch a star or two, no matter what. So she slipped out the window and started off by herself to see if she could reach them.

She walked a long, long time, and then farther still, until she came to a mill wheel, creaking and grinding away.

"Good evening," she said to the mill wheel. "I would like to play with the stars in the sky. Have you seen any near here?"

"Ah, yes," groaned the old mill wheel. "Every night they shine in my face from the surface of this pond until I cannot sleep. Jump in, my lass, and you will find them."

The little girl jumped into the pond and swam around until her arms were so tired she could swim no longer, but she could not find any stars.

"Excuse me," she called to the old mill wheel, "but I don't believe there are any stars here after all!"

"Well, there certainly were before you jumped in and stirred the water up," the mill wheel called back. So she climbed out and dried herself off as best she could, and set out again across the fields.

After a while she sat down to rest in a meadow, and it must have been a fairy meadow, because before she knew it a hundred little fairies came scampering out to dance on the grass.

"Good evening, Little Folk," said the girl. "I'm trying to reach the stars in the sky. Have you seen any near here?"

"Ah, yes," sang the fairies. "They glisten every night among the blades of grass. Come and dance with us, little lass, and you will find as many stars as you like."

So the child danced and danced, she whirled round and round in a ring with the Little Folk, but though the grass gleamed beneath her feet, she never spied a single star. Finally she could dance no longer, and she plopped down inside the ring of fairies.

"I've tried and I've tried, but I can't seem to reach the stars down here," she cried. "If you don't help me, I'll never find any to play with."

The fairies all whispered together. Finally one of them crept up and took her by the hand, and said: "If you're really determined, you must go forward. Keep going forward, and mind you take the right road. Ask Four Feet to carry you to No Feet At All, and then tell No Feet At All to carry you to the Stairs Without Steps, and if you climb that—"

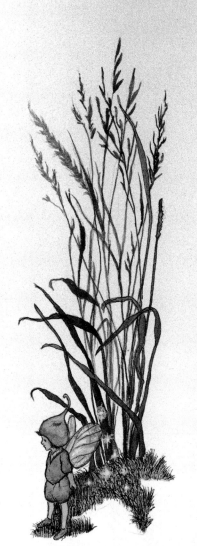

So the little girl set out again with a light heart, and by and by she came to a horse, tied to a tree.

"Good evening," she said. "I'm trying to reach the stars in the sky, and I've come so far my bones are aching. Will you give me a ride?"

"I don't know anything about stars in the sky," the horse replied. "I'm here only to do the bidding of the Little Folk."

"But I come from the Little Folk, and they said to tell Four Feet to carry me to No Feet At All."

"Four Feet? That's me!" the horse whinnied. "Jump up and ride with me."

They rode and they rode and they rode, till they rode out of the forest and found themselves at the edge of the sea.

"I've brought you to the end of the land, and that's as much as Four Feet can do," said the horse. "Now I must get home to my own folk."

So the little girl slid down and walked along the sea, wondering what in the world she would do next, until suddenly the biggest fish she'd ever seen came swimming up to her feet.

"Good evening," she said to the fish. "I'm trying to reach the stars in the sky. Can you help me?"

"I'm afraid I can't," gurgled the fish, "unless, of course, you bring me word from the Little Folk."

"But I do," she cried. "They said Four Feet would bring me to No Feet At All, and then No Feet At All would carry me to the Stairs Without Steps."

"Ah, well," said the fish, "that's all right then. Get on my back and hold on tight."

And off he went—kerplash!—into the water, swimming along a silver path that glistened on the surface and seemed to stretch toward the end of the sea, where the water met the sky. There, in the distance, the little girl saw a beautiful rainbow rising out of the ocean and into the heavens, shining with all the colors.

At last they came to the foot of it, and she saw the rainbow was really a broad bright road, sloping up and away into the sky, and at the far, far end of it she could see wee shining things dancing about.

"I can go no farther," said the fish. "Here are the Stairs Without Steps. Climb up, if you can, but hold on tight. These stairs were never meant for little lassies' feet, you know." So the little girl jumped off No Feet's back, and off he splashed through the water.

She climbed and she climbed and she climbed up the rainbow. It wasn't easy. Every time she took one step, she seemed to slide back two. And even though she climbed until the sea was far below, the stars in the sky looked farther away than ever.

"But I won't give up," she told herself. "I've come so far, I can't go back."

Up and up she went. The air grew colder and colder, but the sky turned brighter and brighter, and finally she could tell she was nearing the stars.

"I'm almost there!" she cried.

And sure enough, suddenly she reached the very tip-top of the rainbow. Everywhere she looked, the stars were turning and dancing. They raced up and down, and back and forth, and spun in a thousand colors around her.

"I'm finally here," she whispered to herself. She had never seen anything so beautiful before, and she stood gazing and wondering at the heavens.

But after a while she realized she was shivering with cold, and when she looked down into the darkness, she could no longer see the earth. She wondered where her own home was, so far away, but no streetlamps or window lights marked the blackness below. She began to feel a little dizzy.

"I won't go until I touch one star," she told herself, and she stood on her toes and stretched her arms as high as she could. She reached farther and farther—and suddenly a shooting star zipped by and surprised her so much she lost her balance.

Down she slid—down—down—down the rainbow. The farther she slid, the warmer it grew, and the warmer it grew, the sleepier she felt. She gave a great yawn, and a small sigh, and before she knew it, she was fast asleep.

When she woke up, she found herself in her very own bed. The sun was peeking through her window, and the morning birds sang in the bushes and trees.

"Did I really touch the stars?" she asked herself. "Or was it only a dream?"

Then she felt something in her hand. When she opened her fist, a tiny light flashed in her palm, and at once was gone, and she smiled because she knew it was a speck of stardust.

RESPONSIBILITY
WORK
SELF-DISCIPLINE

Little Fred

In which we learn how to retire for the evening.

When little Fred
    Was called to bed,
He always acted right;
    He kissed Mama,
    And then Papa,
And wished them all good night.

    He made no noise,
    Like naughty boys,
But gently up the stairs
    Directly went,
    When he was sent,
And always said his prayers.

There Was a Little Girl

In this poem, we see what happens to us sometimes when we do not behave!

There was a little girl,
And she had a little curl
Right in the middle of her forehead.
When she was good
She was very, very good,
And when she was bad she was horrid.

One day she went upstairs,
When her parents, unawares,
In the kitchen were occupied with meals,
And she stood upon her head
In her little trundle-bed,
And then began hooraying with her heels.

Her mother heard the noise,
And she thought it was the boys
A-playing at a combat in the attic;
But when she climbed the stair,
And found Jemima there,
She took and she did scold her most emphatic.

PLEASE

ALICIA ASPINWALL

Good children learn good manners (sometimes from their brothers and sisters).

There was once a little word named "Please" that lived in a small boy's mouth. Pleases live in everybody's mouth, though people often forget they are there.

Now, all Pleases, to be kept strong and happy, should be taken out of the mouth very often, so they can get air. They are like little fish in a bowl, you know, that come popping up to the top of the water to breathe.

The Please I am going to tell you about lived in the mouth of a boy named Dick; but only once in a long while did it have a chance to get out. For Dick, I am sorry to say, was a rude little boy; he hardly ever remembered to say "Please."

"Give me some bread! I want some water! Give me that book!"—that is the way he would ask for things.

His father and mother felt very bad about this. And as for the poor Please itself, it would sit up on the roof of the boy's mouth day after day, hoping for a chance to get out. It was growing weaker and weaker every day.

This boy Dick had a brother, John. Now, John was older than Dick—he was almost ten; and he was just as polite as Dick was rude. So his Please had plenty of fresh air, and was strong and happy.

One day at breakfast, Dick's Please felt that he must have some fresh air, even if he had to run away. So out he ran—out of Dick's mouth—and took a long breath. Then he crept across the table and jumped into John's mouth!

The Please-who-lived-there was very angry.

"Get out!" he cried. "You don't belong here! This is *my* mouth!"

"I know it," replied Dick's Please. "I live over there in that brother's mouth. But alas! I am not happy there. I am never used. I never get a breath of fresh air! I thought you might be willing to let me stay here for a day or so—until I felt stronger."

"Why, certainly," said the other Please, kindly. "I understand. Stay, of course; and when my master uses me, we will both go out together. He is kind, and I am sure he would not mind saying 'Please' twice. Stay as long as you like."

That noon, at dinner, John wanted some butter; and this is what he said:

"Father, will you pass me the butter, please—please?"

"Certainly," said the father. "But why be so *very* polite?"

John did not answer. He was turning to his mother, and said, "Mother, will you give me a muffin, please—please?"

His mother laughed.

"You shall have the muffin, dear; but why do you say 'please' twice?"

"I don't know," answered John. "The words seem just to jump out, somehow. Katie, please—please, some water!"

This time, John was almost frightened.

"Well, well," said his father, "there is no harm done. One can't be too 'pleasing' in this world."

All this time little Dick had been calling, "Give me an egg! I want some milk. Give me a spoon!" in the rude way he had. But now he stopped and listened to his brother. He thought it would be fun to try to talk like John; so he began, "Mother, will you give me a muffin, m-m-m-?"

He was trying to say "please," but how could he? He

never guessed that his own little Please was sitting in John's mouth. So he tried again, and asked for the butter.

"Mother, will you pass me the butter, m-m-m-?"

That was all he could say.

So it went on all day, and everyone wondered what was the matter with those two boys. When night came, they were both so tired, and Dick was so cross, that their mother sent them to bed very early.

But the next morning, no sooner had they sat down to breakfast than Dick's Please ran home again. He had had so much fresh air the day before that now he was feeling quite strong and happy. And the very next moment, he had another airing, for Dick said, "Father, will you cut my orange, please?" Why! the word slipped out as easily as could be! It sounded just as well as when John said it— John was saying only one "please" this morning. And from that time on, little Dick was just as polite as his brother.

Boy Wanted

FRANK CRANE

This "want ad" appeared in the early part of this century.

WANTED–A boy who stands straight, sits straight, acts straight and talks straight;

A boy whose fingernails are not in mourning, whose ears are clean, whose shoes are polished, whose clothes are brushed, whose hair is combed, and whose teeth are well cared for;

A boy who listens carefully when he is spoken to, who asks questions when he does not understand, and does not ask questions about things that are none of his business;

A boy who moves quickly and makes as little noise about it as possible;

A boy who whistles in the street, but does not whistle where he ought to keep still;

A boy who looks cheerful, has a ready smile for everybody, and never sulks;

A boy who is polite to every man and respectful to every woman and girl;

A boy who does not smoke cigarettes and has no desire to learn how;

A boy who is more eager to know how to speak good English than to talk slang;

A boy who neither bullies other boys nor allows other boys to bully him;

A boy who, when he does not know a thing, says, "I don't know," and when he has made a mistake says, "I'm sorry," and when he is asked to do a thing says, "I'll try";

A boy who looks you right in the eye and tells the truth every time;

A boy who is eager to read good books;

A boy who would rather put in his spare time at the YMCA gymnasium than gamble for pennies in a back room;

A boy who does not want to be "smart" or in any wise to attract attention;

A boy who would rather lose his job or be expelled from school than tell a lie or be a cad;

A boy whom other boys like;

A boy who is at ease in the company of girls;

A boy who is not sorry for himself, and not forever thinking and talking about himself;

A boy who is friendly with his mother, and more intimate with her than anyone else;

A boy who makes you feel good when he is around;

A boy who is not goody-goody, a prig, or a little pharisee, but just healthy, happy, and full of life.

This boy is wanted everywhere. The family wants him, the school wants him, the office wants him, the boys want him, the girls want him, all creation wants him.

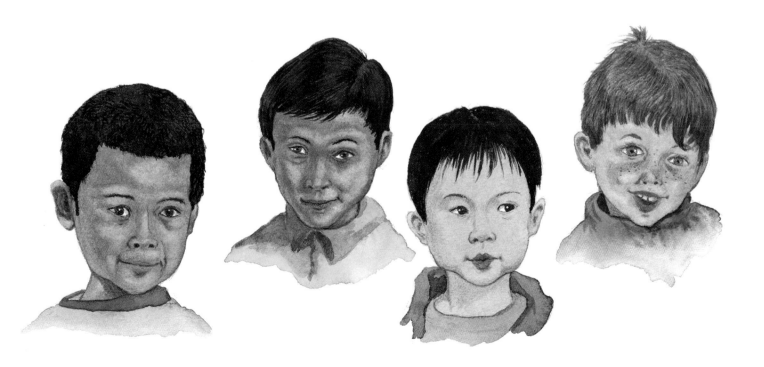

Over in the Meadow

OLIVE A. WADSWORTH

Parents show responsibility by caring for their children. Children show responsibility by listening to their parents.

Over in the meadow,
    In the sand, in the sun,
Lived an old mother toad
    And her little toadie one.
"Wink," said the mother;
    "I wink," said the one;
So she winked and she blinked
    In the sand, in the sun.

Over in the meadow,
    Where the stream runs blue,
Lived an old mother fish
    And her little fishes two.
"Swim," said the mother;
    "We swim," said the two;
So they swam and they leaped
    Where the stream runs blue.

Over in the meadow,
  In a hole in a tree,
Lived an old mother bluebird
  And her little birdies three.
"Sing," said the mother;
  "We sing," said the three;
So they sang and were glad,
  In the hole in the tree.

Over in the meadow,
  In the reeds on the shore,
Lived a mother muskrat
  And her little ratties four.
"Dive," said the mother;
  "We dive," said the four;
So they dived and they burrowed
  In the reeds on the shore.

The Little Red Hen

☞ RETOLD BY PENRYHN W. COUSSENS

If we want a share of the rewards, we must take a share of the work, too.

A little red hen once found a grain of wheat. "Who will plant this wheat?" she says.

"I won't," says the dog.

"I won't," says the cat.

"I won't," says the pig.

"I won't," says the turkey.

"Then I will," says the little red hen. "Cluck! cluck!"

So she planted the grain of wheat. Very soon the wheat began to grow and the green leaves came out of the ground. The sun shone and the rain fell and the wheat kept on growing until it was tall, strong, and ripe.

"Who will reap this wheat?" says the little red hen.

"I won't," says the dog.

"I won't," says the cat.

"I won't," says the pig.

"I won't," says the turkey.

"I will, then," says the little red hen. "Cluck! cluck!"

So she reaped the wheat.

"Who will thresh this wheat?" says the little red hen.

"I won't," says the dog.

"I won't," says the cat.

"I won't," says the pig.

"I won't," says the turkey.

"I will, then," says the little red hen. "Cluck! cluck!"

So she threshed the wheat.

"Who will take this wheat to mill to have it ground?" says the little red hen.

"I won't," says the dog.

"I won't," says the cat.

"I won't," says the pig.

"I won't," says the turkey.

"I will, then," says the little red hen. "Cluck! cluck!"

So she took the wheat to mill, and by and by she came back with the flour.

"Who will bake this flour?" says the little red hen.

"I won't," says the dog.

"I won't," says the cat.

"I won't," says the pig.

"I won't," says the turkey.

"I will, then," says the little red hen. "Cluck! cluck!"

So she baked the flour and made a loaf of bread.

"Who will eat this bread?" says the little red hen.

"I will," says the dog.

"I will," says the cat.

"I will," says the pig.

"I will," says the turkey.

"No, *I* will," says the little red hen. "Cluck! cluck!"

And she ate up the loaf of bread.

The King and His Hawk

RETOLD BY JAMES BALDWIN

Thomas Jefferson once advised us about how to control our temper: When angry, count to ten before you do anything, and when very angry, count to a hundred. Genghis Khan learned the same lesson eight hundred years ago. His empire stretched from eastern Europe to the Sea of Japan.

Genghis Khan was a great king and warrior.

He led his army into China and Persia, and he conquered many lands. In every country, men told about his daring deeds, and they said that since Alexander the Great there had been no king like him.

One morning when he was home from the wars, he rode out into the woods to have a day's sport. Many of his friends were with him. They rode out gaily, carrying their bows and arrows. Behind them came the servants with the hounds.

It was a merry hunting party. The woods rang with their shouts and laughter. They expected to carry much game home in the evening.

On the king's wrist sat his favorite hawk, for in those days hawks were trained to hunt. At a word from their masters they would fly high up into the air, and look around for prey. If they chanced to see a deer or a rabbit, they would swoop down upon it swift as any arrow.

All day long Genghis Khan and his huntsmen rode through the woods. But they did not find as much game as they expected.

Toward evening they started for home. The king had often ridden through the woods, and he knew all the paths. So while the rest of the party took the nearest way, he went by a longer road through a valley between two mountains.

The day had been warm, and the king was very thirsty. His pet hawk had left his wrist and flown away. It would be sure to find its way home.

The king rode slowly along. He had once seen a spring of clear water near this pathway. If he could only find it now! But the hot days of summer had dried up all the mountain brooks.

At last, to his joy, he saw some water trickling down over the edge of a rock. He knew that there was a spring farther up. In the wet season, a swift stream of water always poured down here, but now it came only one drop at a time.

The king leaped from his horse. He took a little silver cup from his hunting bag. He held it so as to catch the slowly falling drops.

It took a long time to fill the cup; the king was so thirsty that he could hardly wait. At last it was nearly full. He put the cup to his lips, and was about to drink.

All at once there was a whirring sound in the air, and the cup was knocked from his hands. The water was all spilled upon the ground.

The king looked up to see who had done this thing. It was his pet hawk.

The hawk flew back and forth a few times, and then alighted among the rocks by the spring.

The king picked up the cup, and again held it to catch the trickling drops.

This time he did not wait so long. When the cup was half full, he lifted it toward his mouth. But before it had touched his lips, the hawk swooped down again, and knocked it from his hands.

And now the king began to grow angry. He tried again, and for the third time the hawk kept him from drinking. The king was now very angry indeed.

"How do you dare to act so?" he cried. "If I had you in my hands, I would wring your neck!"

Then he filled the cup again. But before he tried to drink, he drew his sword.

"Now, Sir Hawk," he said, "this is the last time."

He had hardly spoken before the hawk swooped down and knocked the cup from his hand. But the king was looking for this. With a quick sweep of the sword he struck the bird as it passed.

The next moment the poor hawk lay bleeding and dying at its master's feet.

"That is what you get for your pains," said Genghis Khan.

But when he looked for his cup, he found that it had fallen between two rocks, where he could not reach it.

"At any rate, I will have a drink from that spring," he said to himself.

With that he began to climb the steep bank to the place from which the water trickled. It was hard work, and the higher he climbed, the thirstier he became.

At last he reached the place. There indeed was a pool of water; but what was that lying in the pool, and almost filling it? It was a huge, dead snake of the most poisonous kind.

The king stopped. He forgot his thirst. He thought only of the poor dead bird lying on the ground below him.

"The hawk saved my life!" he cried, "and how did I repay him? He was my best friend, and I have killed him."

He clambered down the bank. He took the bird up gently, and laid it in his hunting bag. Then he mounted his horse and rode swiftly home. He said to himself, "I have learned a sad lesson today, and that is, never to do anything in anger."

Hercules and the Wagoner

☞ A E S O P

This old fable helps us learn early that the only certain labor is our own.

Awagoner was driving his team along a muddy lane with a full load behind them, when the wheels of his wagon sank so deep in the mire that no efforts of his horses could move them. As he stood there, looking help-lessly on, and calling loudly at intervals upon Hercules for assistance, the god himself appeared, and said to him, "Put your shoulder to the wheel, man, and goad on your horses, and then you may call on Hercules to assist you. If you won't lift a finger to help yourself, you can't expect Hercules or anyone else to come to your aid."

Heaven helps those who help themselves.

St. George and the Dragon

RETOLD BY J. BERG ESENWEIN
AND MARIETTA STOCKARD

"Somewhere perhaps there is trouble and fear," St. George says in this story before riding off to "find work which only a knight can do." Such people who go out of their way to help are sometimes called knights, saints; sometimes they are called ministers, teachers, and parents.

Long ago, when the knights lived in the land, there was one knight whose name was Sir George. He was not only braver than all the rest, but he was so noble, kind, and good that the people came to call him Saint George.

No robbers ever dared to trouble the people who lived near his castle, and all the wild animals were killed or driven away, so the little children could play even in the woods without being afraid.

One day St. George rode throughout the country. Everywhere he saw the men busy at their work in the fields, the women singing at work in their homes, and the little children shouting at their play.

"These people are all safe and happy. They need me no more," said St. George.

"But somewhere perhaps there is trouble and fear. There may be someplace where little children cannot play in safety, some woman may have been carried away from her home—perhaps there are even dragons left to be slain. Tomorrow I shall ride away and never stop until I find work which only a knight can do."

Early the next morning St. George put on his helmet and all his shining armor, and fastened his sword at his side. Then he mounted his great white horse and rode out from his castle gate. Down the steep, rough road he went, sitting straight and tall, and looking brave and strong as a knight should look.

On through the little village at the foot of the hill and

out across the country he rode. Everywhere he saw rich fields filled with waving grain, everywhere there was peace and plenty.

He rode on and on until at last he came into a part of the country he had never seen before. He noticed that there were no men working in the fields. The houses which he passed stood silent and empty. The grass along the roadside was scorched as if a fire had passed over it. A field of wheat was all trampled and burned.

St. George drew up his horse, and looked carefully about him. Everywhere there was silence and desolation. "What can be the dreadful thing that has driven all the people from their homes? I must find out, and give them help if I can," he said.

But there was no one to ask, so St. George rode forward until at last far in the distance he saw the walls of a city. "Here surely I shall find someone who can tell me the cause of all this," he said, so he rode more swiftly toward the city.

Just then the great gate opened and St. George saw
crowds of people standing inside the wall. Some of them
were weeping, all of them seemed afraid. As St. George
watched, he saw a beautiful maiden dressed in white, with
a girdle of scarlet about her waist, pass through the gate
alone. The gate clanged shut and the maiden walked along
the road, weeping bitterly. She did not see St. George,
who was riding quickly toward her.

"Maiden, why do you weep?" he asked as he reached her side.

She looked up at St. George sitting there on his horse, straight and tall and beautiful. "Oh, Sir Knight!" she cried, "ride quickly from this place. You know not the danger you are in!"

"Danger!" said St. George. "Do you think a knight would flee from danger? Besides, you, a fair girl, are here alone. Think you a knight would leave you so? Tell me your trouble that I may help you."

"No! No!" she cried, "hasten away. You would only lose your life. There is a terrible dragon near. He may come at any moment. One breath would destroy you if he found you here. Go! Go quickly!"

"Tell me more of this," said St. George sternly. "Why are you here alone to meet this dragon? Are there no men left in yon city?"

"Oh," said the maiden, "my father, the King, is old and feeble. He has only me to help him take care of his people. This terrible dragon has driven them from their homes, carried away their cattle, and ruined their crops. They have all come within the walls of the city for safety. For weeks now the dragon has come to the very gates of the city. We have been forced to give him two sheep each day for his breakfast.

"Yesterday there were no sheep left to give, so he said that unless a young maiden were given him today he would break down the walls and destroy the city. The people cried to my father to save them, but he could do nothing. I am going to give myself to the dragon. Perhaps if he has me, the Princess, he may spare our people."

"Lead the way, brave Princess. Show me where this monster may be found."

When the Princess saw St. George's flashing eyes and great, strong arm as he drew forth his sword, she felt afraid no more. Turning, she led the way to a shining pool.

"There's where he stays," she whispered. "See, the water moves. He is waking."

St. George saw the head of the dragon lifted from the pool. Fold on fold he rose from the water. When he saw St. George he gave a roar of rage and plunged toward him. The smoke and flames flew from his nostrils, and he opened his great jaws as if to swallow both the knight and his horse.

St. George shouted and, waving his sword above his head, rode at the dragon. Quick and hard came the blows from St. George's sword. It was a terrible battle.

At last the dragon was wounded. He roared with pain and plunged at St. George, opening his great mouth close to the brave knight's head.

St. George looked carefully, then struck with all his strength straight down through the dragon's throat, and the dragon fell at the horse's feet—dead.

Then St. George shouted for joy at his victory. He called to the Princess. She came and stood beside him.

"Give me the girdle from about your waist, O Princess," said St. George.

The Princess gave him her girdle and St. George bound it around the dragon's neck, and they pulled the dragon after them by that little silken ribbon back to the city so that all of the people could see that the dragon could never harm them again.

When they saw St. George bringing the Princess back in safety and knew that the dragon was slain, they threw open the gates of the city and sent up great shouts of joy.

The King heard them and came out from his palace to see why the people were shouting.

When he saw his daughter safe he was the happiest of them all.

"O brave knight," he said, "I am old and weak. Stay here and help me guard my people from harm."

"I'll stay as long as ever you have need of me," St. George answered.

So he lived in the palace and helped the old King take care of his people, and when the old King died, St. George was made King in his stead. The people felt happy and safe so long as they had such a brave and good man for their King.

COMPASSION
FAITH

A Child's Prayer

Prayer, like all good habits, is best learned while we are very young.

Lord, teach a little child to pray,
    And then accept my prayer;
For thou canst hear the words I say,
    For thou art everywhere.

A little sparrow cannot fall
    Unnoticed, Lord, by thee;
And though I am so young and small,
    Thou dost take care of me.

Teach me to do the thing that's right,
    And when I sin, forgive;
And make it still my chief delight
    To serve thee while I live.

Kindness to Animals

Think of all creatures great and small.

Little children, never give
Pain to things that feel and live;
Let the gentle robin come
For the crumbs you save at home;
As his meat you throw along
He'll repay you with a song.
Never hurt the timid hare
Peeping from her green grass lair,
Let her come and sport and play
On the lawn at close of day.
The little lark goes soaring high
To the bright windows of the sky,
Singing as if 'twere always spring,
And fluttering on an untired wing—
Oh! let him sing his happy song,
Nor do these gentle creatures wrong.

The Sermon to the Birds

☞ RETOLD BY JAMES BALDWIN

St. Francis was born 800 years ago in Italy. He is still admired for his simple life of poverty, his love of peace, and his respect for all living things.

Very kind and loving was St. Francis—kind and loving not only to men but to all living things. He spoke of the birds as his little brothers of the air, and he could never bear to see them harmed.

At Christmastime he scattered crumbs of bread under the trees, so that the tiny creatures could feast and be happy.

Once when a boy gave him a pair of doves which he had snared, St. Francis had a nest made for them, and the mother bird laid her eggs in it.

By and by, the eggs hatched, and a nestful of young doves grew up. They were so tame that they sat on the shoulders of St. Francis and ate from his hand.

And many other stories are told of this man's great love and pity for the timid creatures which lived in the fields and woods.

One day as he was walking among the trees the birds saw him and flew down to greet him. They sang their sweetest songs to show how much they loved him. Then, when they saw that he was about to speak, they nestled softly in the grass and listened.

"O little birds," he said, "I love you, for you are my brothers and sisters of the air. Let me tell you something, my little brothers, my little sisters: You ought always to love God and praise Him.

"For think what He has given you. He has given you wings with which to fly through the air. He has given you clothing both warm and beautiful. He has given you the air in which to move and have homes.

"And think of this, O little brothers: you sow not, neither do you reap, for God feeds you. He gives you the rivers and the brooks from which to drink. He gives you the mountains and the valleys where you may rest. He gives you the trees in which to build your nests.

"You toil not, neither do you spin, yet God takes care of you and your little ones. It must be, then, that He loves you. So, do not be ungrateful, but sing His praises and thank Him for his goodness toward you."

Then the saint stopped speaking and looked around him. All the birds sprang up joyfully. They spread their wings and opened their mouths to show that they understood his words.

And when he had blessed them, all began to sing; and the whole forest was filled with sweetness and joy because of their wonderful melodies.

Someone Sees You

Faith tells us that no act goes unseen. We are likely to act better with such faith.

Once upon a time a man decided to sneak into his neighbor's fields and steal some wheat. "If I take just a little from each field, no one will notice," he told himself, "but it will all add up to a nice pile of wheat for me." So he waited for the darkest night, when thick clouds lay over the moon, and he crept out of his house. He took his youngest daughter with him.

"Daughter," he whispered, "you must stand guard, and call out if anyone sees me."

The man stole into the first field to begin reaping, and before long the child called out, "Father, someone sees you!"

The man looked all around, but he saw no one, so he gathered his stolen wheat and moved on to a second field.

"Father, someone sees you!" the child cried again.

The man stopped and looked all around, but once again he saw no one. He gathered more wheat, and moved to a third field.

A little while passed, and the daughter cried out, "Father, someone sees you!"

Once more the man stopped his work and looked in every direction, but he saw no one at all, so he bundled his wheat and crept into the last field.

"Father, someone sees you!" the child called again.

The man stopped his reaping, looked all around, and once again saw no one. "Why in the world do you keep saying someone sees me?" he angrily asked his daughter. "I've looked everywhere, and I don't see anyone."

"Father," murmured the child, "Someone sees you from above."

The Honest Disciple

As this Jewish folktale reminds us, faith is often the path to other virtues (in this case, honesty).

Once a rabbi decided to test the honesty of his disciples, so he called them together and posed a question.

"What would you do if you were walking along and found a purse full of money lying in the road?" he asked.

"I'd return it to its owner," said one disciple.

"His answer comes so quickly, I must wonder if he really means it," the rabbi thought.

"I'd keep the money if nobody saw me find it," said another.

"He has a frank tongue, but a wicked heart," the rabbi told himself.

"Well, Rabbi," said a third disciple, "to be honest, I believe I'd be tempted to keep it. So I would pray to God that He give me the strength to resist such temptation and do the right thing."

"Aha!" thought the rabbi. "Here is the man I would trust."

Little Sunshine

 RETOLD BY ETTA AUSTIN BLAISDELL
AND MARY FRANCES BLAISDELL

Bestowing compassion is like offering most other gifts. Often it's the thought that counts.

Once there was a little girl named Elsa. She had a very old grandmother, with white hair, and wrinkles all over her face.

Elsa's father had a large house that stood on a hill.

Each day the sun peeped in at the south windows. It made everything look bright and beautiful.

The grandmother lived on the north side of the house. The sun never came to her room.

One day Elsa said to her father, "Why doesn't the sun peep into Grandma's room? I know she would like to have him."

"The sun cannot look in at the north windows," said her father.

"Then let us turn the house around, Papa."

"It is much too large for that," said her father.

"Will Grandma never have any sunshine in her room?" asked Elsa.

"Of course not, my child, unless you can carry some to her."

After that Elsa tried and tried to think how she could carry the sunshine to her grandmother.

When she played in the fields she saw the grass and the flowers nodding their heads. The birds sang sweetly as they flew from tree to tree.

Everything seemed to say, "We love the sun. We love the bright, warm sun."

"Grandma would love it, too," thought the child. "I must take some to her."

When she was in the garden one morning she felt the sun's warm rays in her golden hair. Then she sat down and she saw them in her lap.

"I will take them in my dress," she thought, "and carry them to Grandma's room." So she jumped up and ran into the house.

"Look, Grandma, Look! I have some sunshine for you," she cried. And she opened her dress, but there was not a ray to be seen.

"It peeps out of your eyes, my child," said her grandmother, "and it shines in your sunny, golden hair. I do not need the sun when I have you with me."

Elsa did not understand how the sun could peep out of her eyes. But she was glad to make her dear grandmother happy.

Every morning she played in the garden. Then she ran to her grandmother's room to carry the sunshine in her eyes and hair.

The Lion and the Mouse

☞ AESOP

With kindness, the smallest can often help the biggest.

One day a great lion lay asleep in the sunshine. A little mouse ran across his paw and wakened him. The great lion was just going to eat him up when the little mouse cried, "Oh, please, let me go, sir. Some day I may help you."

The lion laughed at the thought that the little mouse could be of any use to him. But he was a good-natured lion, and he set the mouse free.

Not long after, the lion was caught in a net. He tugged and pulled with all his might, but the ropes were too strong. Then he roared loudly. The little mouse heard him, and ran to the spot.

"Be still, dear Lion, and I will set you free. I will gnaw the ropes."

With his sharp little teeth, the mouse cut the ropes, and the lion came out of the net.

"You laughed at me once," said the mouse. "You thought I was too little to do you a good turn. But see, you owe your life to a poor little mouse."

The Legend of the Dipper

☞ RETOLD BY J. BERG ESENWEIN
AND MARIETTA STOCKARD

A kind act is often its own reward.

There had been no rain in the land for a very long time. It was so hot and dry that the flowers were withered, the grass was parched and brown, and even the big, strong trees were dying. The water dried up in the creeks and rivers, the wells were dry, the fountains stopped bubbling. The cows, the dogs, the horses, the birds, and all the people were so thirsty! Everyone felt uncomfortable and sick.

There was one little girl whose mother grew very ill. "Oh," said the little girl, "if I can only find some water for my mother I'm sure she will be well again. I must find some water."

So she took a tin cup and started out in search of water. By and by she found a tiny little spring away up on a mountainside. It was almost dry. The water dropped, dropped, ever so slowly from under the rock. The little girl held her cup carefully and caught the drops. She waited and waited a long, long time until the cup was full of water. Then she started down the mountain holding the cup very carefully, for she didn't want to spill a single drop.

On the way she passed a poor little dog. He could
hardly drag himself along. He was panting for breath and
his tongue hung from his mouth because it was so dry and
parched.

"Oh, you poor little dog," said the little girl, "you are so
thirsty. I can't pass you without giving you a few drops of
water. If I give you just a little there will still be enough for
my mother."

So the little girl poured some water into her hand and
held it down for the little dog. He lapped it up quickly and
then he felt so much better that he frisked and barked and
seemed almost to say, "Thank you, little girl." And the little
girl didn't notice—but her tin dipper had changed into a
silver dipper and was just as full of water as it had been
before.

She thought about her mother and hurried along as fast as she could go. When she reached home it was late in the afternoon, almost dark. The little girl pushed the door open and hurried up to her mother's room. When she came into the room the old servant who helped the little girl and her mother, and had been working hard all day taking care of the sick woman, came to the door. She was so tired and so thirsty that she couldn't even speak to the little girl.

"Do give her some water," said the mother. "She has worked hard all day and she needs it much more than I do."

So the little girl held the cup to her lips and the old servant drank some of the water. She felt stronger and better right away and she went over to the mother and lifted her up. The little girl didn't notice that the cup had changed into a gold cup and was just as full of water as it was before!

Then she held the cup to her mother's lips and she drank and drank. Oh, she felt so much better! When she had finished there was still some water left in the cup. The little girl was just raising it to her own lips when there came a knock at the door. The servant opened it and there stood a stranger. He was very pale and all covered with dust from traveling. "I am thirsty," he said. "Won't you give me a little water?"

The little girl said, "Why, certainly I will, I am sure that you need it far more than I do. Drink it all."

The stranger smiled and took the dipper in his hand, and as he took it, it changed into a diamond dipper. He turned it upside down and all the water spilled out and sank into the ground. And where it spilled a fountain bubbled up. The cool water flowed and splashed—enough for the people and all the animals in the whole land to have all the water they wanted to drink.

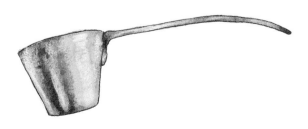

As they watched the water they forgot the stranger, but presently when they looked he was gone. They thought they could see him just vanishing in the sky—and there in the sky, clear and high, shone the diamond dipper. It shines up there yet, and reminds people of the little girl who was kind and unselfish. It is called the Big Dipper.

HONESTY
LOYALTY
FRIENDSHIP

The Pasture

ROBERT FROST

*This little poem reminds us that a friend is
someone we want to be with.*

I'm going out to clean the pasture spring;
I'll only stop to rake the leaves away
(And wait to watch the water clear, I may):
I sha'n't be gone long.—You come too.

I'm going out to fetch the little calf
That's standing by the mother. It's so young,
It totters when she licks it with her tongue.
I sha'n't be long.—You come too.

George Washington and the Cherry Tree

☞ ADAPTED FROM J. BERG ESENWEIN
AND MARIETTA STOCKARD

*Here is the most famous American story about telling the truth.
We should all be like young George.*

When George Washington was a little boy he lived
on a farm in Virginia. His father taught him to ride, and he
used to take young George about the farm with him so that
his son might learn how to take care of the fields and horses
and cattle when he grew older.

Mr. Washington had planted an orchard of fine fruit
trees. There were apple trees, peach trees, pear trees, plum
trees, and cherry trees. Once, a particularly fine cherry tree
was sent to him from across the ocean. Mr. Washington
planted it on the edge of the orchard. He told everyone on
the farm to watch it carefully to see that it was not broken
or hurt in any way.

It grew well and one spring it was covered with white
blossoms. Mr. Washington was pleased to think he would
soon have cherries from the little tree.

Just about this time, George was given a shiny new hatchet. George took it and went about chopping sticks, hacking into the rails of fences, and cutting whatever else he passed. At last he came to the edge of the orchard, and thinking only of how well his hatchet could cut, he chopped into the little cherry tree. The bark was soft, and it cut so easily that George chopped the tree right down, and then went on with his play.

That evening when Mr. Washington came from inspecting the farm, he sent his horse to the stable and walked down to the orchard to look at his cherry tree. He stood in amazement when he saw how it was cut. Who would have dared do such a thing? He asked everyone, but no one could tell him anything about it.

Just then George passed by.

"George," his father called in an angry voice, "do you know who killed my cherry tree?"

This was a tough question, and George staggered under it for a moment, but quickly recovered.

"I cannot tell a lie, father," he said. "I did it with my hatchet."

Mr. Washington looked at George. The boy's face was white, but he looked straight into his father's eyes.

"Go into the house, son," said Mr. Washington sternly.

George went into the library and waited for his father. He was very unhappy and very much ashamed. He knew he had been foolish and thoughtless and that his father was right to be displeased.

Soon, Mr. Washington came into the room. "Come here, my boy," he said.

George went over to his father. Mr. Washington looked at him long and steadily.

"Tell me, son, why did you cut the tree?"

"I was playing and I did not think—" George stammered.

"And now the tree will die. We shall never have any cherries from it. But worse than that, you have failed to take care of the tree when I asked you to do so."

George's head was bent and his cheeks were red from shame.

"I am sorry, father," he said.

Mr. Washington put his hand on the boy's shoulder. "Look at me," he said. "I am sorry to have lost my cherry tree, but I am glad that you were brave enough to tell me the truth. I would rather have you truthful and brave than to have a whole orchard full of the finest cherry trees. Never forget that, my son."

George Washington never did forget. To the end of his life he was just as brave and honorable as he was that day as a little boy.

God Make My Life a Little Light

M. BENTHAM-EDWARDSTHAT

Friends give of themselves.

God make my life a little light,
  Within the world to glow;
A tiny flame that burneth bright
  Wherever I may go.

God make my life a little flower,
  That giveth joy to all,
Content to bloom in native bower,
  Although its place be small.

God make my life a little staff,
  Whereon the weak may rest,
That so what health and strength I have
  May serve my neighbors best.

The Indian Cinderella

☞ RETOLD BY CYRUS MACMILLAN

This Native American tale from Canada is about how honesty is rewarded and dishonesty punished. Glooskap, mentioned in the opening paragraph, was a god of the Eastern woodlands Indians.

On the shores of a wide bay on the Atlantic coast there dwelt in old times a great Indian warrior. It was said that he had been one of Glooskap's best helpers and friends, and that he had done for him many wonderful deeds. But that, no man knows. He had, however, a very wonderful and strange power: he could make himself invisible. He could thus mingle unseen with his enemies and listen to their plots. He was known among the people as Strong Wind, the Invisible. He dwelt with his sister in a tent near the sea, and his sister helped him greatly in his work. Many maidens would have been glad to marry him, and he was much sought after because of his mighty deeds; and it was known that Strong Wind would marry the first maiden who could see him as he came home at night. Many made the trial, but it was a long time before one succeeded. Strong Wind used a clever trick to test the truthfulness of all who sought to win him.

Each evening as the day went down, his sister walked on the beach with any girl who wished to make the trial. His sister could always see him, but no one else could see him. And as he came home from work in the twilight, his sister, as she saw him drawing near, would ask the girl who sought him, "Do you see him?" And each girl would falsely answer "Yes." And his sister would ask, "With what does he draw his sled?" And each girl would answer, "With the hide of a moose," or "With a pole," or "With a great cord." And then his sister would know that they all had lied, for their answers were mere guesses. And many tried and lied and failed, for Strong Wind would not marry any who were untruthful.

There lived in the village a great chief who had three daughters. Their mother had long been dead. One of these was much younger than the others. She was very beautiful and gentle and well beloved by all, and for that reason her older sisters were very jealous of her charms and treated her very cruelly. They clothed her in rags that she might be ugly; and they cut off her long black hair; and they burned her face with coals from the fire that she might be scarred and disfigured. And they lied to their father, telling him that she had done these things herself. But the girl was patient and kept her gentle heart and went gladly about her work.

Like other girls, the chief's two eldest daughters tried to win Strong Wind. One evening, as the day went down, they walked on the shore with Strong Wind's sister and waited for his coming. Soon he came home from his day's work, drawing his sled. And his sister asked as usual, "Do you see him?" And each one, lying, answered "Yes." And she asked, "Of what is his shoulder strap made?" And each, guessing, said "Of rawhide." Then they entered the tent where they hoped to see Strong Wind eating his supper; and when he took off his coat and his moccasins they could see them, but more than these they saw nothing. And Strong Wind knew that they had lied, and he kept himself from their sight, and they went home dismayed.

One day the chief's youngest daughter with her rags and burned face resolved to seek Strong Wind. She patched her clothes with bits of birch bark from the trees, and put on the few little ornaments she possessed, and went forth to try to see the Invisible One as all the other girls of the village had done before. And her sisters laughed at her and called her "fool." And as she passed along the road all the people laughed at her because of her tattered frock and her burned face, but silently she went her way.

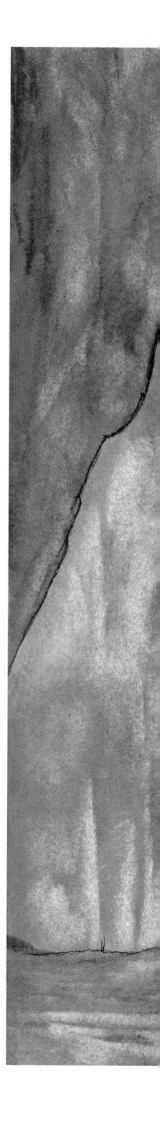

Strong Wind's sister received the girl kindly, and at twilight she took her to the beach. Soon Strong Wind came home drawing his sled. And his sister asked, "Do you see him?" And the girl answered "No," and his sister wondered greatly because she spoke the truth. And again she asked, "Do you see him now?" And the girl answered, "Yes, and he is very wonderful." And she asked, "With what does he draw his sled?" And the girl answered, "With the Rainbow," and she was much afraid. And she asked further, "Of what is his bowstring?" And the girl answered, "His bowstring is the Milky Way."

Then Strong Wind's sister knew that because the girl had spoken the truth at first her brother had made himself visible to her. And she said, "Truly, you have seen him." And she took the girl home and bathed her, and all the scars disappeared from her face and body; and her hair grew long and black again like the raven's wing; and she gave her fine clothes to wear and many rich ornaments. Then she bade her take the wife's seat in the tent. Soon Strong Wind entered and sat beside her, and called her his bride.

The very next day she became his wife, and ever afterward she helped him to do great deeds. The girl's two elder sisters were very cross and they wondered greatly at what had taken place. But Strong Wind, who knew of their cruelty, resolved to punish them. Using his great power, he changed them both into aspen trees and rooted them in the earth. And since that day the leaves of the aspen have always trembled, and they shiver in fear at the approach of Strong Wind; it matters not how softly he comes, for they are still mindful of his great power and anger because of their lies and their cruelty to their sister long ago.

Little Boy Blue

Eugene Field

Some of our earliest, most faithful friends are our childhood toys. May we all learn to be as steadfast in our loyalties as the companions of Little Boy Blue.

The little toy dog is covered with dust,
But sturdy and stanch he stands;
And the little toy soldier is red with rust,
And his musket molds in his hands.
Time was when the little toy dog was new
And the soldier was passing fair;
And that was the time when our Little Boy Blue
Kissed them and put them there.

"Now, don't you go till I come," he said,
"And don't you make any noise!"
So, toddling off to his trundle-bed,
He dreamed of the pretty toys;
And as he was dreaming, an angel song
Awakened our Little Boy Blue—
Oh! the years are many, the years are long,
But the little toy friends are true!

Aye, faithful to Little Boy Blue they stand,
Each in the same old place—
Awaiting the touch of a little hand,
And the smile of a little face;
And they wonder, as waiting these long years through
In the dust of that little chair,
What has become of our Little Boy Blue,
Since he kissed them and put them there.

The Boy Who Cried "Wolf"

Aesop

The fastest way to lose what we call our good character is to lose our honesty.

There was once a shepherd boy who kept his flock at a little distance from the village. Once he thought he would play a trick on the villagers and have some fun at their expense. So he ran toward the village crying out, with all his might: "Wolf! Wolf! Come and help! The wolves are at my lambs!"

The kind villagers left their work and ran to the field to help him. But when they got there the boy laughed at them for their pains; there was no wolf there.

Still another day the boy tried the same trick, and the villagers came running to help and were laughed at again.

Then one day a wolf did break into the fold and began killing the lambs. In great fright, the boy ran back for help. "Wolf! Wolf!" he screamed. "There is a wolf in the flock! Help!"

The villagers heard him, but they thought it was another mean trick; no one paid the least attention, or went near him. And the shepherd boy lost all his sheep.

That is the kind of thing that happens to people who lie: even when they do tell the truth they will not be believed.

The Honest Woodman

☞ ADAPTED FROM EMILIE POULSSON

This old fable, told around the world, shows us that honesty pays.

Once upon a time, out in the green, silent woods near a rushing river that foamed and sparkled as it hurried along, there lived a poor woodcutter who worked hard to make a living for his family. Every day he would trudge into the forest with his strong, sharp axe over his shoulder. He always whistled happily as he went, because he was thinking that as long as he had his health and his axe, he could earn enough to buy all the bread his family needed.

One day he was cutting a large oak tree near the riverside. The chips flew fast at every stroke, and the sound of the ringing axe echoed through the forest so clearly you might have thought a dozen wood choppers were at work that day.

By and by the woodman thought he would rest awhile. He leaned his axe against the tree and turned to sit down, but he tripped over an old, gnarled root, and before he could catch it, his axe slid down the bank and into the river!

The poor woodman gazed into the stream, trying to see the bottom, but it was far too deep there. The river flowed over the lost treasure just as merrily as before.

"What will I do?" the woodman cried. "I've lost my axe! How will I feed my children now?"

Just as he finished speaking, up from the lake rose a beautiful lady. She was the water fairy of the river, and came to the surface when she heard his sad voice.

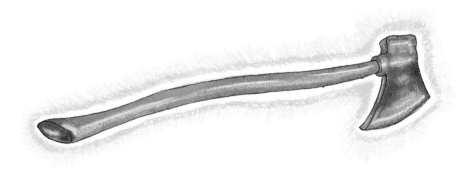

"What is your sorrow?" she asked kindly. The wood-man told her about his trouble, and at once she sank beneath the surface, and reappeared in a moment with an axe made of silver.

"Is this the axe you lost?" she asked.

The woodman thought of all the fine things he could buy for his children with that silver! But the axe wasn't his, so he shook his head, and answered, "My axe was only made of steel."

The water fairy lay the silver axe on the bank, and sank into the river again. In a moment she rose and showed the woodman another axe. "Perhaps this one is yours?" she asked.

The woodman looked. "Oh, no!" he replied. "This one is made of gold! It's worth many times more than mine."

The water fairy lay the golden axe on the bank. Once again she sank. Up she rose. This time she held the missing axe.

"That is mine!" The woodman cried. "That is surely my old axe!"

"It is yours," said the water fairy, "and so are these other two now. They are gifts from the river, because you have told the truth."

And that evening the woodman trudged home with all three axes on his shoulder, whistling happily as he thought of all the good things they would bring for his family.

Why Frog and Snake Never Play Together

This African folktale makes us think about how much companionship the world has missed because people are told they "can't" be friends with each other.

Once upon a time, the child of the Frog was hopping along in the bush when he spied someone new lying across the path before him. This someone was long and slender, and his skin seemed to shine with all the colors of the rainbow.

"Hello there," called Frog-child. "What are you doing lying here in the path?"

"Just warming myself in the sun," answered the some-one new, twisting and turning and uncoiling himself. "My name is Snake-child. What's yours?"

"I'm Frog-child. Would you like to play with me?"

So Frog-child and Snake-child played together all morning long in the bush.

"Watch what I can do," said Frog-child, and he hopped high into the air. "I'll teach you how, if you want," he offered.

So he taught Snake-child how to hop, and together they hopped up and down the path through the bush.

"Now watch what I can do," said Snake-child, and he crawled on his belly straight up the trunk of a tall tree. "I'll teach you if you want."

So he taught Frog-child how to slide on his belly and climb into trees.

After a while they both grew hungry and decided to go home for lunch, but they promised each other to meet again the next day.

"Thanks for teaching me how to hop," called Snake-child.

"Thanks for teaching me how to crawl up trees," called Frog-child.

Then they each went home.

"Look what I can do, Mother!" cried Frog-child, crawling on his belly.

"Where did you learn how to do that?" his mother asked.

"Snake-child taught me," he answered. "We played together in the bush this morning. He's my new friend."

"Don't you know the Snake family is a bad family?" his mother asked. "They have poison in their teeth. Don't ever let me catch you playing with one of them again. And don't let me see you crawling on your belly, either. It isn't proper."

Meanwhile, Snake-child went home and hopped up and down for his mother to see

"Who taught you to do that?" she asked.

"Frog-child did," he said. "He's my new friend.'

"What foolishness," said his mother. "Don't you know we've been on bad terms with the Frog family for longer than anyone can remember? The next time you play with Frog-child, catch him and eat him up. And stop that hopping. It isn't our custom."

So the next morning when Frog-child met Snake-child in the bush, he kept his distance

"I'm afraid I can't go crawling with you today," he called, hopping back a hop or two.

Snake-child eyed him quietly, remembering what his mother had told him. "If he gets too close, I'll spring at him and eat him," he thought. But then he remembered how much fun they had had together, and how nice Frog-child had been to teach him how to hop. So he sighed sadly to himself and slid away into the bush.

And from that day onward, Frog-child and Snake-child never played together again. But they often sat alone in the sun, each thinking about their one day of friendship.